W9-AGT-896

Regina Public Library
BOOK SALE ITEM
Non-returnable

DINO-MIKE

AND THE
UNDERWATER DINOSAURS

WRITTEN & ILLUSTRATED BY FRANCO

STONE ARCH BOOKS
a capstone imprint

Dino-Mike! is published by
Stone Arch Books,
a Capstone imprint
1710 Roe Crest Drive
North Mankato, Minnesota 56003
www.capstoneyoungreader.com

Copyright © 2015 by Stone Arch Books

All rights reserved. No part of this
publication may be reproduced in whole or
in part, or stored in a retrieval system,
or transmitted in any form or by any
means, electronic, mechanical, photocopying,
recording, or otherwise, without written
permission of the publisher.

Cataloging-in-Publication Data is available on
the Library of Congress website.

ISBN: 978-1-4342-9629-0 (library binding)
ISBN: 978-1-4965-0167-7 (eBook)
ISBN: 978-1-4342-9633-7 (paperback)

Summary: Dino-Mike is headed to an
underwater dinosaur habitat in this chapter
book adventure!

Printed in Canada
042016   009752R

CONTENTS

Young Michael Evans travels the world with his dino-huntin' dad. From the Jurassic Coast in Great Britain to the Liaoning Province in China, young Dino-Mike has been there, *dug* that!

When his dad is dusting fossils, Mike's boning up on his own dino skills — only he's finding the real deal. A live T. rex egg! A portal to the Jurassic Age!! An undersea dinosaur sanctuary!!!

Prepare yourself for another wild and wacky Dino-Mike adventure, which nobody will ever believe . . .

Chapter 1

SUB SURPRISE

Tiny little bubbles popped on the surface of the ocean. They soon grew bigger and bigger. **POP! POP! POP!**

Suddenly, the dome of a high-tech submarine rose out of the water.

Mike and his dad watched as the vessel docked near them in the harbor. Then the hatch opened . . .

"Hi!" exclaimed Shannon. Her red
hair glowed against the gray-blue sub.
"Ready for our underwater adventure?"

Shannon bounced off the submarine
and onto the dock. She grabbed Mike's
dad's hand and shook it firmly. "How are
you today, Dr. Evans?" she asked.

"Very well, Shannon. Excited about the trip," replied Mike's dad.

"Then let's not waste any time!" she said. "All aboard!"

Mike and his dad climbed the ladder of the submarine. The ocean wind made for a chilly morning. Mike was glad he had on his Dino Jacket. The special coat was keeping him warm and toasty.

When they reached the deck, Shannon turned to Mike and his father. "I'd like to introduce you to Captain Vitcus Whitall," she said.

A tall man in a red naval uniform extended his hand.

"You must be Mike Evans," said the man. He gave Mike a curious stare. "Welcome aboard the *Atlantica*."

Captain Whitall turned back to Shannon. "Shall we make preparations to get underway, Ms. Shannon?" he said.

"Please," she responded.

The captain bowed at Shannon's request. Then he gestured to two men dressed in matching red uniforms. They opened a nearby hatch. Shannon led the way as Mike and his dad followed.

"Is your dad on board?" Mike's dad asked Shannon.

"No," said Shannon. "He rarely leaves our home on the ocean floor."

Mike couldn't blame his dad for being curious. Even to him, Shannon was still a complete mystery. He'd been in life-or-death situations capturing dinosaurs with this girl, and he'd only recently started to learn about her.

Then, out of the blue, Shannon had invited him and his dad to her underwater home. Mike hoped she'd finally reveal some secrets, and he hoped to reveal some of his own. Mike hadn't told his father about the real dinos he had discovered several weeks earlier.

Once the hatch closed, the captain angrily barked orders at his crew.

"Captain Whitall?" Shannon said. "Could I take Mike on a sub tour?"

"Certainly. If you would like, I could conduct the tour," offered the captain.

"That's not necessary, but maybe you could entertain Dr. Evans," she replied.

"My pleasure, sir. This way." Captain Whitall gestured down a corridor. Before leaving, he turned to Shannon. "Ms. Shannon, I'll send the steward down with some refreshments for you."

"Thank you, Captain," said Shannon.

Mike followed Shannon through the twisting tunnels of the ship. Soon, they emerged into a giant entertainment room. On one wall was a flat-screen television with three different video game systems.

"This is incredible!" Mike exclaimed.

"Yeah, the ocean can get pretty boring," explained Shannon.

"Now you have me to keep you company," said Mike.

Shannon blushed. "Thanks," she said. "I'm glad you're here. You've been so much help. I want to explain everything: the T. rex, the dinosaur eggs, and my brother."

"Ugh," interrupted Mike. "If there's one person I never want to see again, it's your brother, Jurassic Jeff."

"Did someone say my name?" came a voice from behind them.

Mike turned. He couldn't believe his eyes.

Chapter 2

JURASSIC JEFF

Jurassic Jeff was holding a tray with drinks and snacks on it. He was also wearing a red uniform that matched the rest of the crew.

"W-what is he doing here?" Mike exclaimed. "Why is he not locked up?"

"He's my brother," Shannon replied. "No matter what he's done, he's family."

"Thank you," replied Jeff, putting the tray on the table.

"But that doesn't mean he's off the hook," Shannon explained. "My dad grounded him."

"Grounded?" said Mike, surprised.

"He doesn't look grounded."

Jeff straightened his uniform. "Obviously, you don't know what it's like working for Captain Whitall," he said. "He's the most demanding captain to ever sail the seas!"

"It's true," agreed Shannon. "My father hired him because he demands respect and hard work from his crew."

"I've never worked so hard in my life!" said Jeff, plopping down on a couch. "We're building a large, watertight containment area near the back of the ship. I also run around doing all sorts of errands, like bringing you refreshments. It's humiliating!"

Jeff unfastened the top button of his uniform and took a cookie from his tray. He put his feet up on the coffee table and bit into the cookie. Just as Jeff was starting to relax, the voice of the captain boomed over the intercom.

"Broome!" shouted Captain Whitall.

Jeff leaped off the couch. "Uh, yes? Yes, sir?" said Jeff, spitting out remnants of the cookie.

"Bring our guests to the command center," demanded the captain. "On the double!"

"Yes, sir, Captain, sir," Jeff replied.

Jeff motioned for Mike and Shannon to follow him. "Come on!" he yelled. "We don't want to make him mad!"

Jeff led the duo through the maze of the ship. He didn't waste time getting them to the command center.

The minute Captain Whitall was in view, Jeff snapped to attention. He saluted and exclaimed, "Sir, Mike and Shannon are here. As you ordered, sir."

"What took you so long, recruit?" shouted the captain.

"You certainly run a tight ship, Captain," Mike's dad commented.

"There is no room on a seagoing vessel for insubordination, Dr. Evans," replied Captain Whitall. "We need discipline. The only job this crew has is to follow my orders.

"But enough chit-chat. Let's discuss the real reason for your visit."

The captain nodded to a recruit seated nearby at a computer station. The recruit pushed a button on a high-tech control panel. The roof of the submarine opened, revealing a large glass dome. Mike looked out at the dark ocean. In the distance, a building glowed.

"Welcome to Atlantis," said Shannon.

Chapter 3
ATLANTIS

As the submarine approached the underwater complex, two large doors opened to a tunnel. The captain piloted the sub inside, eventually surfacing in a large docking facility.

The *Atlantica* docked between two other submarines. Then the hatch opened, and they began to disembark.

The captain had the entire crew assemble on the deck. He ordered Jeff to bring down Mike and his father's bags.

Just then, a door at the far end of the dock opened like an automatic garage door. A tall, thin man with bushy hair and a zebra-striped lab coat approached the group.

The man stopped a few feet from them. "Hello," he said.

Shannon left Mike's side, bounced over to the man, and gave him a big hug. "Hi, Daddy!"

"Hello, my dear," he answered back and then looked at Mike and his father. He bent slightly and whispered to Shannon, "Are we sure about this?"

Shannon took her father by the hand and led him the few extra feet toward Mike. "Yes," she answered him. "Dad, this is Mike and his father, Dr. Evans."

"Hello. Pleasure to meet you," he said as he shook hands with them.

"Likewise," said Mike's dad. "I've studied so much of your research that you're like an old friend, Dr. Broome."

"Well, it's a pleasure to meet such a well-read man." Dr. Broome laughed.

"No problems on the voyage?" he asked, eyeing his son, Jeff.

"No, Doctor," answered the captain. "The trip was . . . uneventful."

"Good! Good!" said Dr. Broome. He turned and gestured for Mike and his dad to follow. "Then let me give you a tour of the facilities."

As he led the way, Dr. Broome put his arm around Shannon. "I'm still not entirely sure about bringing strangers here," he whispered.

Shannon smiled and whispered back, "Don't worry, Dad. I trust Mike."

Dr. Broome leaned over and kissed his daughter on the forehead. "If you say so, dear. You can show him the holding pens and the feeders but not the portal room. He doesn't need to see that."

Then he turned to Mike's father. "Dr. Evans, why don't we let the kids explore? Besides, I'm sure they don't want to be saddled with two old fossils like us."

Mike's dad laughed at the joke, and then asked, "And us?"

"We'll head to my lab on the other side of the complex," said Dr. Broome. "It's specially designed with reinforced soundproof walls, state of the art computer systems, and one of the most power telescopes on Earth!"

"A telescope? Underwater?" asked Mike's dad, amazed.

"Oh, yes!" answered Dr. Broome. "I have many passions: paleontology, archeology, and astronomy."

Mike's father turned to his son and said, "Be on your best behavior, buddy!"

Mike smiled and waved at his dad. "You got it, Dad!"

The adults walked away excitedly. The rest of the crew disappeared into the submarine, along with Jeff and Captain Whitall, leaving just Shannon and Mike on the dock.

Shannon smiled at Mike and asked, "Ready to see some dinosaurs?"

Chapter 4

DIFFERENT DINOS

"This is incredible, Shannon!" said Mike. He watched Parasaurolophus dinosaurs from outside an large pen.

"These dinosaurs are recovering from injuries," explained Shannon.

"How was this built?" asked Mike. "We're thousands of feet under water and this place has trees, grass, and sun!"

"That sun is a solar lamp," Shannon told Mike. "A really, REALLY big one."

"Still, how is this all possible?" Mike asked again. "And where did the dinosaurs come from?"

Shannon hesitated and then began, "Years ago, my dad came here to study underwater dinosaur fossils. But shortly after arriving, he discovered a mysterious cave. When he entered, he found a trapped pocket of air with a perfectly preserved prehistoric world. The cave had everything: plants, trees, and even dinosaurs!"

"But how?!" asked Mike eagerly.

"Many believe this area was once home to the lost city of Atlantis," explained Shannon. "My dad built this facility to study the dinosaurs and find out for sure."

"What about Sam, the T. rex we captured on our last adventure?" asked Mike. "Is she here? I'd love to see her!"

"She was here," Shannon began. "But after running loose on land, we had to do some testing to make sure she and her babies were okay. They are being kept in quarantine."

Shannon pointed to a door at the far end of the holding pen.

Mike could see a large, bolted door made of reinforced metal. A red light glowed above the door and a sign read, *DO NOT ENTER*.

"That's the only place I'm not allowed to take you," said Shannon.

"I was kind of hoping to see her," said Mike, disappointed.

"Don't worry," said Shannon. "There are plenty of other dinosaurs." She typed a secret code into a keypad, and the door to the dinosaur pen opened. "Now zip up your jacket. It's cold in there."

"Really?" he asked. "We can go in?"

"Sure, I do it all the time," said Shannon. "Besides, Parasaurolophus are herbivores, harmless plant eaters."

"I k-know," said Mike, nervous.

Shannon and Mike entered the enclosed pen. It was large, with wide-open spaces and plenty of plants and trees for the Parasaurolophus to feed on.

Once Mike calmed down, he felt the chill in the air and zipped up his Dino Jacket. The jacket had been a present from his dad. Over the past few weeks, the high-tech jacket had become something he depended on.

Mike moved closer to the herd of
Parasaurolophus feeding on the leaves
of a nearby tree. When they didn't
run away, he reached out a hand and
touched one. It still didn't run. With his
hand on the creature, Mike could feel it
breathing in and out. Dino-Mike felt like
he was part of the herd.

Suddenly, Mike felt the muscles underneath his hand tense. Dino-Mike realized that everything had become eerily silent. The entire herd stopped moving. They were all still and alert, not making a sound.

"W-what's happening?" he asked Shannon.

"We should run," replied Shannon.

"What? Why?" asked Mike.

ROOOOAAAARRRRRRRRR!

Mike and Shannon turned around. Standing on the wall of the holding pen were two very hungry Troodon!

Chapter 5

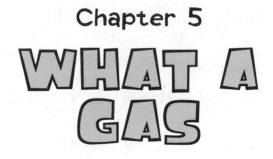

The Troodon rushed at Shannon and Mike. Then the nearby Parasaurolophus started to stampede. Danger was coming at them from both sides!

Thinking fast, Dino-Mike pulled the hood of his Dino Jacket over his head. Two bright lights on the hood glowed like the eyes of a Tyrannosaurus rex.

Then Mike pressed a small, red
button on his sleeve.

ROOOOOOOOARRRRRRR!

The thundering roar of a T. rex
blasted from speakers inside his jacket.
The Parasaurolophus scattered in all
different directions.

"One problem down," said Mike.

"And one to go," added Shannon. She pointed at the angry Trodoons still headed toward them.

Shannon ran to a nearby crate. She lifted the lid and pulled out what looked like a fire extinguisher.

"Hold your breath!" she shouted.

FWOOOOOSH! Shannon blasted the oncoming Troodon with the extinguisher. A burst of green mist sprayed out of the device.

In an instant, the Troodon fell to the ground, asleep. Shannon pulled Mike out of the green cloud.

"Whew!" Shannon exclaimed. "I didn't know if this sleeping gas would work on Troodon. We got lucky!"

"Lucky?" questioned Mike.

"Yes," Shannon replied. "Troodon are probably the smartest dinosaurs of all. They're extremely dangerous."

"What's going on here?" asked Mike. "If your dad found dinosaurs trapped in a cave after all these years, there wouldn't have been so many species."

"What are you talking about?" asked Shannon, puzzled.

"These dinosaurs are from different times!" Mike explained. "The Troodon were from the Mesozoic Era, and the Parasaurolophus were from the Late Cretaceous Period. They never lived together in the same time period, but your dad found them all in the same place? That's impossible. Somebody would've had to bring them together."

"You don't think —?" Shannon began but was afraid to finish.

"Yes," said Mike. "Jurassic Jeff."

Chapter 6
FISH TANK

After securing the Troodon, Mike and Shannon exited the dinosaur pen. They didn't expect what they saw . . .

Dinosaurs everywhere!

Shannon spotted one of the sub's crew members wrestling a baby Triceratops. "What happened?" she shouted at the man.

"We don't know!" the man screamed. "Someone let all the dinosaurs out of their holding pens!"

"How bad is it?" asked Shannon.

"The dinos are contained to this side of the complex," replied the man. "Your dad's research labs are safe."

"Good! Don't alert him yet. Not unless you have to," demanded Shannon. "He has someone from the surface with him, and we'd like this to be kept secret for as long as we can."

"Aye, aye, Ms. Shannon," said the man, giving a quick salute.

Mike was relieved. His dad was safe.

Shannon turned to Mike. "We have to find Jeff and make sure whatever evil plan he's hatched doesn't happen."

"He must have released the dinosaurs to create a distraction," Mike said. Trying to think like Jeff would, Mike asked, "How would you get a dinosaur out of here?"

Then it came to him. "The sub! The *Atlantica*! The docks are on this side of the complex, aren't they?" Mike asked.

"Yes," answered Shannon. "I really thought he wasn't going to do this anymore. Captain Whitall seemed to have him under control."

"I know it's a long shot, but there is the possibility that he had nothing to do with this incident," said Mike.

"I don't think so," Shannon replied. "I know my brother."

Mike and Shannon ran toward the docks. Finally, they reached the basement and burst through the doors.

The large submarine was still docked. Jeff was throwing down his duffle bag from the deck of the *Atlantica*. Mike and Shannon ran toward him as he began to descend the metal ladder.

"JEFF!" screamed Shannon. "How could you?!"

Jeff jumped down onto the dock. "What are you talking about?" he said.

"What are you up to?" Shannon said, getting into his face.

"Uh," said a confused Jeff, "packing my stuff and leaving the ship."

"Just tell me why you did it." Shannon pressed him again.

"Seriously," said Jeff. "I have no idea what you're talking about."

Mike looked down at Jeff's duffel bag. "What's in there?" he asked.

"Not that it's any of your business, Dino-Mike, but they're my clothes."

"So there's else nothing in there?"
Mike pursued. "Dinosaur eggs or live
baby dinosaurs or something?"

"Have you gone crazy?" asked Jeff.

Without asking, Mike snatched Jeff's
duffel bag.

"HEY!" Jeff protested. "What do you think you're doing? That's my stuff!"

To Mike and Shannon's surprise, there was nothing in the duffel bag except clothes, just like Jeff had said.

"Fine. There's nothing in there, but we know you're up to something," said Shannon. "Why else would you release the dinosaurs from their holding pens?"

"What?" Jeff exclaimed. He seemed genuinely shocked. "Someone did that?"

"It wasn't you?" said Shannon, reading the honest reaction in Jeff's face.

"I don't know anything about it," insisted Jeff.

Mike still had his doubts, but then Shannon asked, "Well, if you didn't do it, then who did?"

Jeff shrugged shoulders. "But," he admitted, "it's exactly what I *would* do if I wanted to steal a dinosaur again."

Jeff started to head away from the submarine and back toward the main part of the complex where all the dinosaurs were. "It's the perfect distraction," he continued. "Open all the pens of the herbivores and other less dangerous dinosaurs —"

"Yeah, I don't know about *less* dangerous," interrupted Mike.

"Anyway," Jeff continued, "while everyone else runs around trying to capture them, I could steal one of the bigger ones."

Then Shannon said, "I want to believe you, Jeff, but statements like that make me think that you had everything to do with this!"

Mike agreed with her.

"I've thought about trying to steal a dinosaur," said Jeff. "But the reason I never attempted is because I don't want to hurt Dad — Wait! Dad! Is he okay?"

"Yes," Shannon replied "He's sealed in his research lab, away from all the dinosaurs pens. I don't think he even knows what happened yet."

Jeff looked relieved. Seeing that scared expression made Mike finally believe he was telling the truth. He may be crazy Jurassic Jeff, but he truly didn't want to see his family get hurt.

"Okay," started Mike, "maybe we know *why* someone would do this, but we still don't know *who*. If it's not you, then who is it?"

Suddenly, the sub started moving away from the dock behind them.

"The *Atlantica*!" exclaimed Shannon. "Where's it going?"

Jeff turned around, bewildered by what he was seeing. "It's submerging!"

"Without you?" asked Shannon. "Why aren't you on the sub?"

"Captain Whitall told me to pack my bag because we would be stationed here for a while. He said I didn't have to stay on the ship, and told me I could sleep in my own room on Atlantis."

"Then why is he leaving?" Shannon wondered aloud.

"I don't know," said Jeff. "The captain has been acting kind of weird lately."

"Weird? How?" asked Mike.

"He's been asking a lot of questions about the facility," Jeff explained. "I didn't think anything of it at first, but it seems strange now."

"What else?" pressed Shannon.

"Actually, I think I mentioned it before. He's been sectioning off a large area of the sub. It used to be sleeping quarters, but he's been having us work on making it into a cargo area," Jeff offered up.

"Why?" asked Mike.

"I don't know," said Jeff. "Every time I asked, he would yell at me and tell me to 'just follow orders.' We had just finished water-sealing the entire cargo area. He had engineers make it so the whole back end could open underwater."

"So, he basically had you build a giant fish tank?" asked Mike.

"Yeah," answered Jeff, "big enough to hold a whale."

"Why would he do that?" Mike wondered.

Jeff stared at Shannon with a worried look on his face. As she looked back at him, she became increasingly anxious. They both turned and watched the sub fully submerge and disappear under the surface of the water.

Jeff turned to look at Shannon once again and quietly breathed out just one word: "Kronosaurus."

Chapter 7
KRONOSAURUS

"Are we sure Captain Whitall is trying to steal a dinosaur?" asked Mike.

"It makes sense! He had that large containment area built, and he made sure I wasn't on the sub," said Jeff.

As he ran through the facility with Jeff and Shannon, Mike saw that most of the dinosaurs had been contained.

"How do we know you're not behind all of this and working with the captain?" Mike asked one more time.

"Have you met the captain? Like I have the power to make that man do anything!" Jeff said. "My dad put me to work for him as a punishment, and that's exactly what it was!"

"Then why would he do something like this?" asked Shannon.

"The guy's an egomaniac! Everything was his way or the highway!" offered Jeff. "I'm telling you, he's probably on his way to the Kronos containment field right now!"

They turned a corner and went through the Parasaurolophus pens. The door was marked *DO NOT ENTER! Portal Containment Area — Authorized Personnel Only!*

Mike remembered hearing Shannon's father whisper something about a portal area to her, but he didn't have time to think about that now. They passed several more doors clearly marked *DO NOT ENTER*, which were heavily bolted with lights flashing above each one.

Jeff continued with his theory as they ran. "The Krono is the only thing the captain could be after. He built that cargo area on the ship to hold the Kronosaurus and all the water it needs. We have to stop him!"

They arrived at the end of the corridor and stopped at a bolted hatch.

"If you're right and he's trying to steal this dinosaur, the world is going to find out about it or this place. So why are you helping us?" asked Shannon. "Isn't that what you want too?"

"Well, yeah, kind of," answered Jeff, unlocking and opening the hatch.

Then he said, "I want the world to know about these dinosaurs, but I want to be the one to tell everyone!"

That made sense to Mike in an odd sort of way, but his thoughts quickly turned to the dinosaur. "So you guys have a Kronosaurus here?" he asked.

"Is that so hard to believe after some of the things you've seen?" replied Jeff.

Any doubts Mike had were quickly put to rest when he saw what was behind the massive hatch. He was not expecting this. The area was huge! He couldn't believe it was still part of the same complex.

In giant holding pens were the biggest dinosaurs he had ever seen: Allosaurs, Brachiosaurs, Spinosarus, Shantungosaurus, and Dipolodocus.

Mike was speechless. The only thing he could manage to say was, "Um . . ."

"Impressive, right?" said Jeff.

"H-how did you —? Did these —?" Mike was finally able to ask, "They were all in the caverns your dad discovered?"

"Caverns?" asked Jeff. "What caverns — Wait! That's why he built the containment area in the sub! Whitall doesn't know about the portal. How did he find out about all the dinosaurs?"

Now it was Mike's turn to ask, "Portal?"

"We can discuss all of this later! Right now, let's concentrate on stopping Captain Whitall!" urged Shannon.

"How are we supposed to do that?" asked Mike as he passed holding pen after holding pen of some of the largest dinosaurs to ever roam the Earth.

"He's probably going to bring the sub into the Kronos containment area. He'll need to come up underneath the Kronosaurus and take a whole bunch of water with it! If we close the emergency fence, he won't be able to get in."

They entered another area with a
hatch even bigger than the last one.
Inside was a room with walls made of
glass. *Reinforced glass,* thought Mike,
strong enough to keep out ocean water.

Stepping into the room was like stepping into a large air bubble in the middle of the ocean. They were completely surrounded by water!

"This is it? This is where the Kronosaurus is located?" asked Mike.

"Yup," responded Shannon.

Mike squinted to see if he could spot the beast out in the watery depths. He saw something in the distance that looked like a tiny fish. Then it started to get bigger and bigger and bigger. Mike was getting the feeling that it wasn't a fish after all. It kept coming closer.

It was a Kronosaurus all right!

The Kronosaurus looked like a bunch of different animals smashed together. The beast had the head of a dolphin, alligator teeth and snout, the body of a whale, and the tale of a snake.

"That thing is scarier than a great white shark," Mike mumbled.

"That thing eats great white sharks for breakfast," Shannon explained.

Mike took a step back. The Kronosaurus just floated near the glass wall and stared at him. Maybe the beast was eyeing Mike as his next meal.

"Just be happy you're on this side of the glass," added Jeff.

Then Mike saw a familiar bubble rising up from the depths: the *Atlantica* submarine! The sub dwarfed the huge Kronosaurus. The *Atlantica* skillfully moved into position under the dinosaur and opened its cargo bay doors.

Mike yelled at the sea dinosaur, "GO ON! SHOO! GET OUT OF HERE!"

"Why are you doing jumping jacks?" asked Jeff. "You're only keeping its attention and making it easier for Whitall to capture him!"

"How do we stop him?" asked Mike as he stopped jumping, realizing Jeff was right. By this time, the sub had swallowed the dinosaur into its cargo hold and was closing its hatches.

"Keep your jacket on, Dino-Boy. I got this!" said Jeff.

Jeff pushed a button on a nearby control panel. The power in the room drained, making the lights flicker for a moment before turning back on.

"What did you do?" asked Mike.

"I slammed the cage down around him. It's a stasis field that keeps the Kronosaurus from swimming away, basically like an invisible fence. If the captain tries to escape, he'll fry all the electrical systems on the sub or maybe even destroy it. Captain Whitall is trapped, and he knows it!"

As Jeff was explaining, Mike noticed the sub turning.

"Um, I think he may have found a solution to his problem," Mike said to Jeff and Shannon as he backed further away from the glass.

"What are you talking about?" asked Jeff. Then Jeff saw what was happening. The *Atlantica* had changed course and was heading straight for them!

"He's going to ram us!" shouted Dino-Mike.

Chapter 8

WHAMM!

The nose of the sub smashed into the glass. A spider-web pattern of cracks spread across the entire glass surface.

"We have to get out of here! NOW!" yelled Jeff.

The group rushed out of the room, sealing a giant hatch behind them.

BOOM!! They could hear the sound of thick pieces of glass hitting the wall, followed by the rush of ocean water.

"That guy is crazy!" said Shannon, nearly shocked.

"I could have told you that!" said an exasperated Jeff.

"Is he going to come through the whole complex?" asked Mike, panicked.

"No. The glass is one thing, but the walls of this place are different. My dad built this to withstand underwater earthquakes," said Jeff. "He was probably hoping to flood the room in order to shut down the stasis field!"

"Will it shut down?" asked Mike.

"No. By now he's realized that didn't happen. He's going to have to shut it down from the power core at the center of the facility," Jeff explained.

"He'll need to dock the sub and send someone inside," said Shannon. "We need get to the power core first and make sure that doesn't happen."

"Right!" said Jeff. "But it's going to take two people to get the power turned back on if Whitall or his guys manage to reach the core before us."

"No problem!" said Mike. "There are three of us! Let's get moving."

"Wait! Someone should try to free the Kronosaurus," said Jeff.

"And you think that should be you? Then without any of us watching you can make a getaway with another dinosaur!" said Mike accusingly.

"Actually, I was thinking you could do it," said Jeff.

"I thought so!" exclaimed Mike. "Wait— What?"

"No, it makes sense," said Shannon. "You need to get to the sub while Jeff and I go to the power core. If we do need to get the core running again, we both know how to do that. You don't."

Mike still didn't like the idea. It wasn't the thought of facing scary Captain Whitall and an entire submarine crew by himself that he didn't like. It was Shannon going off alone with Jeff.

He didn't have a choice. "Okay. Let's do this!" Mike finally said.

The complex was mostly empty now. Handlers were probably securing the dinosaurs Whitall and his crew had set free. Mike looked down the long corridor where Dr. Broome's research lab was located. The door was still sealed and had not been breached.

"Don't worry. My dad's lab is more secure than the White House . . . and more soundproof! They have no clue what's going on out here," said Shannon.

They stopped, and Shannon pointed. "Captain Whitall will be docking the ship right through there, where we first came in," she said.

Then Shannon pointed in the opposite direction. "We're going down this way to the power core."

They stared at each other for a moment. Then she hugged Mike hard.

"Good luck," she whispered in his ear. "Thank you for everything!"

Mike hugged her back. "Be careful."

"Come on! He'll be here any minute!" urged Jeff.

Mike watched them go. He took a deep breath and then turned and headed for the docks.

Once on the docks, Mike thought he would have time to figure out a plan to stop the captain, but no such luck.

The *Atlantica* was already docked and Captain Whitall and two crewmembers were descending from the sub. As the three men approached him, Mike decided to stall them. The captain stopped and looked at Mike.

"Michael, correct?" asked Whitall.

"Mike."

"Yes. Of course," said the captain. "Are you the one responsible for blocking our egress?"

"Your what?" asked Mike.

"Our escape. Are you responsible for stopping us from leaving?"

"Yes," answered Mike. "Why are you trying to escape with a Kronosaurus that doesn't belong to you?"

"That's the point. I think everyone should see it. It belongs to the entire world," said the captain.

"But why?" asked Mike.

"I want to be remembered as the man who discovered a real-life sea monster!" said the captain. "The day I spotted that blip on my radar and I found what Dr. Broome was hiding in these waters, I knew my destiny would be complete!"

Mike was shocked. "You're doing this just to be famous?" he asked.

"And the glory that goes with it!" added Whitall.

Mike was never deliberately mean to anyone, but this was a desperate situation. "Wow. We should call you Captain Cashew, because you're nuttier than a squirrel," said Mike.

Mike could tell by the look on the captain's face that he was not happy.

The captain pointed at Mike and yelled at his crew, "Get him!"

The stalling was over. Mike panicked as the two men rushed toward him.

He acted on instinct and pulled the strings on the collar of his Dino Jacket. Flaps emerged from under his arms, just like on a Dilophosaurus dinosaur.

The Dilophosaurus could shoot venom at its prey or an enemy. Mike's Dino Jacket had water that sprayed from the ends of the strings. **SPA-LOOSH!**

Mike's aim had gotten pretty good. He hit both crewmembers in the face with the water, distracting them long enough for Mike to run around them.

How was he going to keep these guys occupied and away from Jeff and Shannon? Mike was running toward the sub when the idea hit him. If he could get on the sub and lock out the captain long enough to disable it, he might be able to save the day.

As he started to climb the ladder on the side of the sub, he heard Captain Whitall yell out, "You two, get to the power core, and shut it down. I'll handle this little problem."

Mike reached the top and could hear the captain climbing up behind him. Dino-Mike jumped into the sub.

Then Mike tried to shut the hatch to the submarine. Suddenly, the hatch was violently ripped open. The captain was much stronger than Mike and easily pulled it open with Mike still hanging on to the lever of the hatch. Mike let go and dropped down to the floor. Not knowing what to do or where to go, he ran down one corridor after another.

A sign above his head read, *ENGINE ROOM*. If Mike could get in there and mess things up, he could stop the captain from getting away.

Then he heard the intercom crackle above his head.

Captain Whitall's booming voice filled the corridors. "Attention all crew! Secure all exits! No one gets in or out! We have a stowaway on board! Make sure he does not leave this vessel!"

Great, thought Mike. *This is exactly what I do not need.*

He kept going toward the engine room. Along the way, he passed by a large area that had been ripped apart. This must be the area Jeff had been working in to build the containment area for the sea dinosaur. It looked like the captain wanted it done in a hurry, because a lot of things were unfinished.

Mike continued running until he reached the door to the engine room and pulled it open. He would get inside, mess up anything he could find, and it would be over.

"Finally!" he said out loud as he stepped inside.

What he did not expect was the ship's mechanic and five other crew members. They all stopped what they were doing and turned to stare at Mike.

The only thing Mike could say was, "Uh-oh."

Chapter 9
MINTY

Two men dragged Mike down the hall. In his mind, Mike was considering all the gadgets inside his Dino Jacket, but he couldn't reach any buttons.

When they neared the end of the hall, the men unlatched a door. They opened it, tossed Mike inside, and then slammed the door behind them.

Mike was trapped.

His only hope was that Shannon and Jeff were able to keep the stasis field up. Then the sub would have no way out, and it would have to stay docked.

Mike looked all around the room. It was someone's bedroom. The bed was unmade, and there were clothes heaped up in a small closet.

There were dinosaur posters, blueprint layouts of Atlantis, and handwritten notes taped all over the walls. On the small desk in the corner of the room were even more papers. Then something caught Mike's attention.

It was brochure he had seen before
— from the Natural History Museum in
New York City. Mike picked it up.

This is the map Jeff had when he
found me and Shannon in New York City,
he thought.

Dino-Mike recognized all the
markings and circles Jeff had made on
it. This was Jeff's room!

Mike searched the desk again. Under the map, he found a small notebook. Leafing through it, he saw all sorts of scribbles and drawings in Jeff's handwriting. He noticed another pile of notebooks and dinosaur books stacked between the desk and the wall.

He looked through some of the books and found that underneath the large pile was a green fire extinguisher.

That's weird, Mike thought. *Why would he have the fire extinguisher buried under books?*

Suddenly, he heard the bolts of the door unlocking.

Mike panicked and stuffed the notebook he was holding into his jacket. Captain Whitall entered the room.

"I tried to warn you, kid. You cannot stop me," he said. "As soon as my men return, we will be on our way, and this game will be finished."

Mike glanced at the open door behind the captain.

Captain Whitall noticed. "Oh, don't worry," he said. "They may not be directly outside the door, but my men are all over the ship. You'd never make it out of here."

Mike's spirits fell. He knew the captain was right.

Captain Whitall smiled. "Now, this thing you did to my men with your jacket. What was that?" he asked.

Mike was cornered. Any trick or gadget he used now would only momentarily distract the captain.

Mike knew he'd never be able get past all the crew members.

"It was just water. It's like a squirt gun," said Mike.

"You children and your toys," replied the captain. "Where did you get it?"

"My father made it for me."

"Ah yes, the paleontologist," said the captain. "Does he know about the sea creature I have in my cargo bay?"

Mike said nothing. Shannon had explained that few people knew about the dinosaurs on Atlantis. The captain may have found Kronosarus, but maybe he didn't know anything else.

"You don't need to keep secrets from me," the captain added. "I know all about the dinosaurs in this facility. I'm not a bad guy. I just want the sea creature. The rest of these dinosaurs can be left alone."

He started to leaf through the notes on Jeff's desk.

"Dr. Broome can keep his precious secrets," the captain continued. "I would never have known about them myself if it wasn't for Jeff. His father insisted he learn discipline by being one of my crew members. He was being punished, but I was never told for what."

Captain Whitall turned to face Mike again. "One day, I happened to stop in here to see young Jeff, and he wasn't in. I came across these papers and drawings." He pointed to everything around the room. "I found quite a number of interesting notes and things. I tell you this because I want you to know I could have done a great deal more, but all I took was this one creature."

Mike was trying to think of a way out of this situation.

Then the intercom crackled with the voice of a crew member. "Captain, we've returned. The stasis field is down."

Mike's heart sank. What happened to Shannon and Jeff? Were they hurt? Mike was thinking the worst.

The captain walked over to the speaker next to the door and pushed a button. "Very good. Secure all hatches and prepare to get underway."

Captain Whitall threw the museum brochure at Jeff's desk. "You might as well get some rest," he told Dino-Mike. "It's a long trip to where we're going."

The brochure slid and landed on the big pile next to the desk, knocking over all of its contents. Mike saw the green fire extinguisher under all the books.

Wait — GREEN? Mike thought.

Mike suddenly realized it wasn't a fire extinguisher at all. It was a canister of dinosaur knockout gas. Jeff had a canister of knockout gas hidden in his room. Mike saw his chance.

He pulled up his hoodie, flipping it onto his head. The two large eyes on the hood illuminated the entire room, blinding the captain. Mike also deployed the T. rex roar. **ROOOOOAR!** Captain Whitall was trying to shield his eyes and cover his ears at the same time.

Mike moved quickly.

He grabbed the green canister and ran for the door. He slammed it shut and tried to lock the captain in.

Captain Whitall had other plans. Recovered from the assault on his eyes and ears, the captain pushed open the door. Mike ran.

For a second, Mike thought about spraying the captain with the knockout gas, but then he had another idea.

Mike stayed just ahead of Captain Whitall as he was trying to remember how to get back to the engine room area. The captain grabbed for him but couldn't hold on because of the slippery scales on Mike's Dino Jacket.

Soon, Mike reached the construction area by the engine room. He turned and confronted the captain, raising the nozzle of the canister at him.

Captain Whitall stopped. "What are you doing?"

Mike began to back up as he spoke. "Stay away from me, or I'll blast you."

"HAHA! With a fire extinguisher?" asked the captain. He advanced slowly toward Mike. "That canister is filled with foam to put out fires. It's not going to hurt me."

Mike backed up until he hit a wall and could go no further.

Seeing this, the captain stood up tall, towering over Mike. "Stop being silly, and hand over that fire extinguisher. It's over. You've lost. Give up."

Mike raised the nozzle and held it as high above his head as he could.

He tried to come up with something clever to say but all he could think of was, "Nope." Then Mike took the deepest breath he could muster and held it. He pulled the trigger on the green canister.

SPOOOOOOOOSHHH!

The knockout gas shot from the nozzle. It was immediately sucked up into the air vent that had been left open after the construction on the cargo bay. Mike was standing right under the vent.

The wide-eyed captain could only watch as the green cloud disappeared. "That's not a fire extinguisher!" he screamed.

Mike just held his breath and kept squeezing the trigger until the canister was empty. The captain looked around in a panic. Green mist was starting to pour from the submarine air vents. It was suddenly everywhere.

"It's in the ship's air system. That stuff is getting pumped into every room on this vessel!" said the captain.

Mike smiled, held his breath, and nodded to the captain. This just made Captain Whitall angrier.

"What did you do, you little . . . " The captain lunged forward in an attempt to grab Mike.

All he could manage were a few steps before he passed out cold on the floor.

Mike did it, but he wasn't out of trouble yet. He jumped over the captain and started running.

Mike held his breath as he ran, finding unconscious crew members everywhere. He finally made it to the ladder and climbed up to the hatch.

Mike tried with all his strength to push it open, but his lungs burned and he needed air. He breathed in.

Mike could taste the green mist. It was surprisingly minty! Unable to hold on, he slid back down the ladder. He reached the floor and found he could no longer stand.

As he lay on the floor, he stared at the hatch above. His eyelids grew heavy, breathing in more of the minty mist.

Suddenly a light appeared. Someone
was opening the hatch from the outside.

His vision was blurry, but Mike could
just make out a person peering in. They
were holding a handkerchief over their
nose and mouth.

He couldn't tell who it was, only that they had red hair.

Mike smiled and closed his eyes.

Chapter 10
A BIG FAVOR

"Shannon?" asked Mike as he fought through a sleepy haze, trying to wake up. He saw the same blurry red-headed figure looking down at him, except this time he wasn't on the floor of the submarine. He was lying down on something soft, not cold and hard.

He was on a bed!

Gradually his focus returned, and Mike realized where he was. He was in a room somewhere on the Atlantis facility. The room was strangely familiar. It was decorated much like Jeff's room on the sub but different. It smelled nice, and it didn't have piles of messy clothes and books all over.

"Shannon?" Mike asked again.

"Easy, son," came a voice from beside him. It was Dr. Broome in his zebra-striped lab coat. He was standing next to the bed. The blurry figure looking down at Mike through the hatch had been Dr. Broome, not Shannon.

"Captain Whitall! He's trying to steal the Kronosaurus! He wants to tell the world about it! We have to stop him!"

Dr. Broome put a hand on Mike's shoulder. "Relax, son. You already stopped him."

"I did?" asked a confused Mike. "I don't remember . . ."

"Well, you did," said Dr. Broome. "You used a canister of my dinosaur knockout gas in the ventilation system of the submarine. You knocked everyone out on the ship, including yourself."

Mike rubbed his head. "Yeah. It was, um, minty."

"Thanks, it's an all-natural recipe. Surprise, the main ingredient is mint leaves!" Dr. Broome smiled. "You did an incredibly brave thing, young man. You almost even made it all the way out of the sub."

"But the captain —" began Mike.

"He's in custody, along with the rest of the crew."

"Wait!" Mike started. "If you're here, where's my dad? Is he okay?"

"Yes, yes, perfectly fine," answered Dr. Broome. "He's in my dinosaur simulator. It's a ride I developed for amusement parks. It's one of a number of ways I generate money to keep this place going. His input will be invaluable in making the ride as authentic as we can make it. After all, he did design that Dino Jacket of yours. We've been bouncing ideas off each other all day."

Mike was relieved. "So, he's okay, and he doesn't know anything about the dinosaurs here?"

"No, he doesn't. I greatly appreciate you keeping my family secret."

Mike swung his feet over the edge of the bed. He looked around the room and realized it was Shannon's room. There was a picture of her and Dr. Broome by the nightstand.

Mike panicked again.

"Where's Shannon?" Mike asked.
"She and Jeff went to make sure the
stasis field wasn't shut off, but the men
came back and —"

"That's where I'm afraid I need to ask
you to do something," said Dr. Broome.

"Oh no!" said Mike. "Is she hurt?"

"No, at least I don't think so," replied Dr. Broome.

"What?" asked Mike. "Where is she?"

"She and Jeff have disappeared."

"Disappeared? How? We're miles underwater. Did you check the power core?" asked Mike.

"From what we can figure out, they never made it to the power core," said Dr. Broome.

"But they said they were going there to make sure it was guarded against Captain Whitall and his men," said Mike.

"Yes, and apparently it was left to you to make sure the captain was stopped. You did that, and I am indebted to you. That is why I should not ask what I'm about to ask," said Dr. Broome. "Are you up for another adventure . . . or rather, a rescue mission?"

"Dr. Broome, what's happened?"

Dr. Broome exhaled. "I'm afraid my son, Jeff, is a dinosaur freak. In his misguided enthusiasm, he wants the entire world to know the thrill of seeing a real live dinosaur."

Mike knew he should never have trusted Jeff. "Did he steal another dinosaur? Did he take a submarine?"

"Jeff has never taken a dinosaur from this facility," said Dr. Broome.

Mike was confused. "What? What about the T. rex he set loose in Montana?"

"That T. rex did not come from this facility," Dr. Broome explained. "The only dinosaurs we have here are injured ones we are nursing back to health. We patch them up and then return them."

"Return them? Doc, where did Jeff take Shannon?" asked Mike, scared to know the answer.

Dr. Broome paused and then said, "Mike, I need you to go back in time . . . to the Jurassic period."

Time for another adventure! thought Dino-Mike.

GLOSSARY

herbivore (HUR-buh-vore)—an animal that eats plants rather than other animals

Jurassic Period (juh-RA-sik PIHR-ee-uhd)—a period of time about 200 to 144 million years ago

paleontologist (pale-ee-uhn-TOL-uh-gist)—a scientist who deals with fossils and other life-forms

prehistoric (pree-hi-STOR-ik)—belonging to a time before history was recorded in written form

triceratops (try-SER-uh-tops)—a large, plant-eating dinosaur with three horns and a fan-shaped collar of bone

tyrannosaurus (ti-RAN-uh-sor-uhs)—a large, meat-eating dinosaur that walked on its hind legs, also known as a T. rex

DINO FACTS!

Troodon dinosaurs survived during the late Cretaceous period, about 76-70 million years ago. Their name, Troodon, means "wounding tooth," and it's no surprise. Their long, serrated teeth made them deadly carivores.

In 1855, geologist Ferdinand V. Hayden discovered the first Troodon fossil in Alberta, Canada.

Parasaurolophus (PAR-a-saw-ROL-o-fus) is a funny dinosaur name to say. This dino also made some funny noises! Parasaurolophus's long, bony crest on its head allowed the dinosaur to sound like a fog horn.

The name Kronosaurus (CROW-no-SORE-us) is Greek for "Kronos lizard."

Kronosaurus is a large example of a pliosaur, marine reptiles characterized by their thick heads, short necks, stocky trunks and outsized flippers. These underwater beasts averaged more than 30 feet long and nearly 10 tons.

Kronosaurus swam much like modern sea turtles, using four paddle-like flippers. Some scientist believe that these dinosaurs, like turtles or seals, could move from the water to land.

ABOUT THE AUTHOR

Bronx, New York–born writer and artist Franco Aureliani has been drawing comics since he could hold a crayon. Currently residing in upstate New York with his wife, Ivette, and son, Nicolas, he spends most of his days in his Batcave-like studio where he works on comics projects. In 1995, Franco founded Blindwolf Studios, an independent art studio where he and fellow creators can create children's comics. Franco is the creator, artist, and writer of Weirdsville, L'il Creeps, and Eagle All Star, ~~~~~~~~~~~~~ator and writer of Pa

Franco re~~~~~~~~~~~~~~~~~~~~~~~~~~~
Superman Far~~~~~~~~~~~~~ now cowriting the ~~~~~~~~~~~~~n: Teen Trillionaires an~~~~~~~~~~~~~omics. When he's not~~~~~~~~~~~~~Franco teaches high s